Wendy was getting her car ready for the race.

GRAND RACE ON WHEELS

1st prize

3

Monkey wanted to take part. "I'm going to win the cake," he said.

"Don't be silly," Wendy said, crossly. "I will win it."

The race began.
Wendy drove off.

The monkey was fast.

He went past Wendy.

Then his wheels fell off.
"Ha, ha!" Wendy shouted.

"I'll win that cake."

She passed him.

Monkey found a scooter.
He rode quickly.

Wendy was far away.
He wanted to catch up
with her car.

Wendy had to stop for
petrol. Monkey laughed.

He rushed past.

And knocked into a tree!

Wendy was going up a hill.
The monkey was on a
skateboard.

A bus passed. The monkey
jumped onto it.

Monkey was at the top of
the hill! "I'm going to win!"

17

Wendy caught up to him.
The monkey went down
the hill very fast.

18

Too fast!

He splashed into the lake!

Wendy was close to the
end of the race.

She went as fast as
she could.

But the monkey was
wearing roller skates.

He caught up with her!

They were both winners!
"Where's the cake?"
Monkey cried.

"I want that cake!"
Wendy shouted.

27

Wendy and Monkey raced for the cake!

29

Puzzle 1

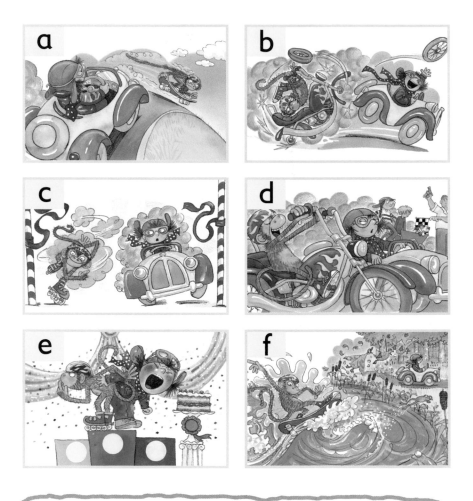

Put these pictures in the correct order.
Now tell the story in your own words.
How short can you make the story?

Puzzle 2

excited   shocked

happy

sad   thrilled

upset

Choose the word which best describes each character. Can you think of any more? Pretend to be one of the characters!

Answers

Puzzle 1

The correct order is:

1d, 2b, 3a, 4f, 5c, 6e

Puzzle 2

Wendy   The correct word is shocked.

The incorrect words are excited, happy.

Monkey   The correct word is thrilled.

The incorrect words are sad, upset.

Look out for more Leapfrog stories:

Mary and the Fairy
ISBN 978 0 7496 9142 4

Pippa and Poppa
ISBN 978 0 7496 9140 0

The Bossy Cockerel
ISBN 978 0 7496 9141 7

The Best Snowman
ISBN 978 0 7496 9143 1

Big Bad Blob
ISBN 978 0 7496 7796 1

Cara's Breakfast
ISBN 978 0 7496 7797 8

Sticky Vickie
ISBN 978 0 7496 7986 6

Handyman Doug
ISBN 978 0 7496 7987 3

The Wrong House
ISBN 978 0 7496 9480 7

Prickly Ballroom
ISBN 978 0 7496 9475 3

That Noise!
ISBN 978 0 7496 9479 1

The Scary Chef's Scarecrow
ISBN 978 0 7496 9476 0

Alex and the Troll
ISBN 978 0 7496 9478 4

The Frog Prince and the Kitten
ISBN 978 1 4451 1614 3*
ISBN 978 1 4451 1620 4

The Animals' Football Cup
ISBN 978 0 7496 9477 7

The Animals' Football Camp
ISBN 978 1 4451 1610 5*
ISBN 978 1 4451 1616 7

Bill's Bouncy Shoes
ISBN 978 0 7496 7990 3

Bill's Scary Backpack
ISBN 978 0 7496 9468 5

Bill's Silly Hat
ISBN 978 1 4451 1611 2*
ISBN 978 1 4451 1617 4

Little Joe's Balloon Race
ISBN 978 0 7496 7989 7

Little Joe's Boat Race
ISBN 978 0 7496 9467 8

Little Joe's Horse Race
ISBN 978 1 4451 1613 6*
ISBN 978 1 4451 1619 8

Felix and the Kitten
ISBN 978 0 7496 7988 0

Felix Takes the Blame
ISBN 978 0 7496 9466 1

Felix, Puss in Boots
ISBN 978 1 4451 1615 0*
ISBN 978 1 4451 1621 1

Cheeky Monkey on Holiday
ISBN 978 0 7496 7991 0

Cheeky Monkey's Treasure Hunt
ISBN 978 0 7496 9465 4

Cheeky Monkey's Big Race
ISBN 978 1 4451 1612 9*
ISBN 978 1 4451 1618 1

For details of all our titles go to: www.franklinwatts.co.uk

*hardback